Hurricane Harry

by JUDITH CASELEY

Greenwillow Books New York

Printed in the United States of America   First Edition   1 2 3 4 5 6 7 8 9 10

Library of Congress Cataloging-in-Publication Data
Caseley, Judith.
    Hurricane Harry / by Judith Caseley.
        p.   cm.
    Summary: Turning five years old, Harry faces the challenges of moving to a new house, acquiring a pet turtle, and starting kindergarten.
    ISBN 0-688-10027-9
    [1. Moving, Household—Fiction.
2. Family life—Fiction.]
I. Title.
PZ7.C2677Hu   1991
[Fic]—dc20
90-13809   CIP   AC

For SCH,
with love

———————

Contents

1
Ride 'em, Hurricane Harry

WHEN HARRY KANE was little, he climbed to the top of the monkey bars and roared so ferociously that the birds flew out of the nearby trees. "He's like a wild animal," his mother said to the lady sitting next to her, but she laughed at the end, so Harry knew it wasn't true. Besides, that day he was pretending he was a lion, Harry Kane, King of the Jungle.

He roared again and his mother called out, "Harry Kane!" very firmly, to make him stop. He pretended he was deaf like Uncle Herman, and his mother repeated "Harry Kane!" even louder. When Harry roared so fiercely that he made a baby cry, his mother cried "Harry Kane!" three times fast, so fast that the boy next to him said, "Is your name really Hurricane?"

"Yes," Harry answered, "Hurricane Harry." He liked the way it sounded . . . fast and funny and ferocious.

When Harry told Grandma Rebecca he was Hurricane Harry, she agreed. "Sometimes you're too fast for your own good," said Grandma when he jumped over the magazine rack and almost knocked down the rubber plant. "Hurricane Harry, you're a terror," Grandma called, but she was smiling, so Harry knew she didn't really mind.

Harry Kane wasn't little anymore, but he still liked to think of himself as Hurricane Harry. He had finished two afternoons a week at Happy Time Nursery, and it was summer. His mother told him that when the swimming stopped and summer was over, he would start kindergarten.

Harry's sister Dorothy had just finished the first

grade, and she was very proud to be entering the second.

"Kindergarten is no big deal," she told Harry. "Not like the second grade. That's real school, where you already know how to read and write and everything."

Harry didn't believe her. After all, he would be at school all day, five days a week, and no lunches with his mother. He thought that was a very big deal.

One day, Harry's mother called them in from the playground outside the window. "They're leaving, Leah," she told her neighbor, an old lady who was keeping an eye on them. "You can take a rest now!" Leah waved and watched while Harry and Dorothy ran into the apartment building and up the stairs.

It was a family conference, and even Chloe was there. Chloe was the oldest, and going into third grade, so she usually got to pick where she sat on the couch. She chose the end by the plump pink cushion. Pink was her favorite color. Dorothy sat in the middle, because she was the middle child, and because she liked keeping Harry and Chloe apart. There was less trouble that way.

The three of them sat quietly. Family conferences were important. The last one they had had was when Grandma was sick in the hospital, and that was a long time ago. She was better now.

Mrs. Kane cleared her throat and said, "We're going to move."

"To a house," said Mr. Kane quickly. "In about a month."

Dorothy and Chloe didn't say a word. But Harry said, "I like our apartment."

"I know you do," said Mrs. Kane gently. "But in the new house you won't have to share a room with Dorothy. You'll have your own room."

"But I sing with Dorothy at night," said Harry.

"He's right," said Dorothy. "We sing a lot."

"You can sing before you go to bed," said Mrs. Kane. "In the new living room."

"But Dorothy keeps me from getting scared," said Harry.

"He's right," said Dorothy. "I do."

"We'll buy you each a nice night-light," said Mr. Kane. "A Mickey Mouse night-light."

"No, thank you," said Harry.

"No, thank you," said Dorothy.

Chloe took her pink pillow and threw it on the floor, just like that. "I won't go," she said. "I won't leave my friends."

"I'm afraid you'll have to," said Mrs. Kane, picking up the pillow. "You'll make new friends."

"We won't go!" said Chloe, and she leaned against Dorothy, and Dorothy leaned against Harry.

"You'll get used to the idea," said Mr. Kane, and he pushed himself out of the armchair. "How about some ice cream?"

No one said a word. Finally, Harry said, "With chocolate sauce?"

"With chocolate sauce," said his father.

"And no Mickey Mouse," said Harry.

"What do you mean?" said Mr. Kane.

"No Mickey Mouse night-light," said Harry. "I

want a light in the shape of a bug."

"And I want Minnie Mouse!" said Dorothy. She looked at Chloe.

"I'm much too old for a night-light," said Chloe. "But I guess I'll have some ice cream with chocolate sauce."

"Chocolate sauce it is," said Mrs. Kane.

"And sprinkles," said Dorothy.

"With a cherry on top!" said Harry.

Mrs. Kane smiled at Mr. Kane. Then they all went into the kitchen and had vanilla ice cream with chocolate sauce and sprinkles and a cherry each on top.

The next day, the family went on an adventure.

"It's a surprise," said Mr. Kane as they piled into the car.

"They're trying to make us feel better," said Chloe. Chloe was usually right. She was smart.

"I'd like a new doll," said Dorothy.

"Forget about it," said Chloe. "They don't work that way."

"A new Transformer?" said Harry.

"No way," said Chloe. "Dad thinks we have too many toys, anyway."

"And they won't want to clutter up the new house," said Dorothy, who was squeezed between Harry and Chloe in the backseat, and was smart, too.

"We're here!" said Mrs. Kane, and they climbed out of the car and stood in front of a white picket fence.

Chloe read the sign. "Applegate Farm. Petting zoo. Rides. Do not feed the animals."

"It's kind of commercial," whispered Mrs. Kane to Mr. Kane.

"One ride apiece," said Mr. Kane, buying them each a ticket.

They followed a path to the petting zoo.

"How come they call it a zoo if it's supposed to be a farm?" said Harry.

"Who knows?" said his father. "Here's a rabbit hutch."

Dorothy put her finger by the wire mesh, but the

rabbits ate lettuce in the corner. So the children gave the rabbits names.

"That one is Harry," said Harry. "He has brown hair like me."

"And that one is Dorothy," said Dorothy. "She's pretty."

"And that one is Chloe," said Chloe, "because she's the biggest."

"Good-bye, Harry. Good-bye, Dorothy. Good-bye, Chloe," they said as they left the rabbits.

"How come they call it a petting zoo if you can't pet them?" asked Harry.

"Who knows?" said his mother. "Here's a goat."

But the goat was busy butting his head against a wall, and he was behind a wire fence, too. Nobody put any fingers out to pet him.

The geese were next. "Geese bite," Mr. Kane warned, prying Harry's fingers off the fence. "This is not a petting zoo."

They listened to the geese honk. They tried honking like them, and Harry's mother said he sounded just like one. Then they left the petting zoo.

"Rides!" shouted Dorothy, pointing to a wooden gate that looked like Lincoln Logs. Some children were standing in line holding tickets, and Chloe and Dorothy and Harry joined the end of it.

"I want to ride the horse!" shouted Harry as he watched a boy with a big cowboy hat climb onto the saddle. Then a man with a mustache led the horse around the corral in a circle.

When their turn came, Chloe went first. She hardly needed any help getting up on the horse and she sat in the saddle, smiling. "It's high up here," she warned Dorothy as the horse trotted down the path.

When it was Dorothy's turn, she wasn't sure if she wanted to get on. "Maybe I'll go on the horse and buggy," she said as she watched Chloe dismount. "He looks a little lonely."

But the man with the mustache hoisted her up before she could say anything. "There you go, little

9

lady," he said, strapping a belt around her. "You're a natural."

To Harry, it looked as if Dorothy gritted her teeth, or even as if she was in the dentist's chair, and he called out, "Is it high?"

Dorothy trotted off without answering.

When the man with the mustache lifted her off, Harry asked her again, "Was it high?"

But Dorothy shrugged her shoulders and straightened her shirt. After all, she was a natural.

It was Harry's turn.

"You're a big boy," said the man as he lifted Harry into the air.

But as one leg sailed over the horse's back, Harry started to wriggle in midair. "No, no," he shouted, "I want the horse and buggy."

"The horse and buggy it is," said the man, and he motioned to a boy with pimples and said, "Get the nag."

The nag was a big horse, too, but he kind of sagged in the middle like an old stuffed animal, and he had white whiskers. He reminded Harry a little of Grandpa Leon. The boy with pimples helped Harry into the buggy and gave him the reins.

"Hold tight," he said, which was silly because the boy held on to the ends of the rope and walked Harry and the horse and buggy so slowly that it was worse than the smallest kiddy ride at McDonald's.

Harry tried to pretend he was riding the horse of a different color in *The Wonderful Wizard of Oz,* but the buggy smelled funny, and it just wasn't the same. He could see his mother and father waving in the distance. He didn't wave back.

When the ride was over, they walked back to the car. Chloe and Dorothy talked about being daredevil riders in the circus. Harry climbed into the back of the car and crammed himself into the corner.

"Why didn't you ride the horse?" said Dorothy. "You would have had much more fun."

"It was great!" said Chloe, the daredevil rider in the other corner. "What happened to you, Hurricane Harry?"

Harry thought for a minute. "I felt sorry for the horse and buggy," he said. "Nobody wanted a ride with him."

"So what?" said Chloe. "You missed something terrific."

"He reminded me of Grandpa," said Harry fiercely.

"Don't let Grandpa know," said Mr. Kane in the front seat. "That horse was about to keel over."

"Harry has a good heart," said his mother kindly.

That night, when Harry's parents were eating popcorn in front of the television, Mrs. Kane heard Dorothy say, "Harry's crying."

"I'll go," said Mr. Kane. He walked into the bedroom and sat on Harry's bed.

"What's the matter, Son?" he said, and he touched Harry's cheek.

Harry cried some more.

"Are you sick?" said Mr. Kane, stroking Harry's hair.

Harry's face was very red. He hiccuped, and said between sobs, "I didn't ride the horse."

"Well, that's okay," said Harry's father. "There will be other times."

"No, there won't!" shouted Harry. "We're moving away."

That's when Harry's father got down on the floor, on his hands and knees, and said, "Ride 'em, cowboy."

After a moment, Harry wiped his eyes on the sheet and climbed on top of his father's back. His father bucked and whinnied and took Hurricane Harry on a trip from the bedroom to the living room and back again.

Chloe and Dorothy stood in the doorway and watched.

"Isn't he getting kind of big for this kind of thing?" called Chloe to her mother in the next room.

"No," her mother called back, and she went right on eating popcorn.

2

Harry's Pet

HARRY SAID GOOD-BYE to his best friend, Joshua, and to Joshua's pet hamster, Pee Wee. It was his last play date with Joshua. It was his last play date with Pee Wee.

When Harry's father drove him home and they walked in the front door, Harry and Mr. Kane didn't smell any dinner. It was Saturday, and Saturday meant roast chicken.

But Harry didn't smell anything.

"I wonder where Mom is," he said to his father.

"I don't know," said Mr. Kane. "Let's play detective."

Harry made believe he had a magnifying glass. "Hmm," said Harry, looking at the floor. "I see a clue."

Mr. Kane held out his pretend magnifying glass. "Aha!" he said. "Newspapers!"

Harry followed the trail of newspapers down the hall. "Follow me," he said to his father. Then he stopped. "Shh," he said. "I hear noises!"

Harry's father cupped his hand around his ear. "Clinking noises!" he whispered back.

They rounded the corner into the kitchen, very quietly.

"Aha!" said Mr. Kane.

"Aha!" said Harry. "We've found you!"

"You scared me!" said Harry's mother. "And I was never lost!" She continued wrapping newspaper around a glass. Then she put the wrapped glass carefully in a box. "Could you hand me some dishes, please?" she said to Mr. Kane.

Mr. Kane took some plates and bowls down from the shelf. They made a clinking noise. "That explains the noises," he said to Harry.

"And that explains the newspapers," said Harry to his father as he watched his mother separate some more sheets of paper. "But what are you doing?"

"I'm packing," said Harry's mother.

"Oh," said Harry sadly. "We're really moving."

"I'm afraid so," said Mrs. Kane. "Did you say good-bye to Joshua?"

"Yes," said Harry, hanging his head. "I'll miss him. And I'll miss Pee Wee, too."

"Of course you will," said Mrs. Kane. "It's hard to leave your friends. It's hard for me to leave, too."

"It is?" said Harry, looking surprised.

"Certainly," said his mother. "You were born here, and so were Dorothy and Chloe. And you know Leah, our neighbor?"

"Sure," said Harry. "She's old."

"When you were a baby," said Mrs. Kane, "I had lunch with Leah every day." His mother looked sad. "Those were nice times," she said.

Harry brightened a little. "She can come and visit!" he said. "And so can Joshua!"

"That's true," said Mrs. Kane, smiling.

"And do you know what else?" said Harry.

"What?" said his mother.

"Joshua can bring Pee Wee with him when he comes to our new house!" Harry had another idea. "And Leah can come at the same time. We can all have lunch together."

"I'm not sure what hamsters eat," said Mrs. Kane.

"Roast chicken," said Harry. "I'm sure Pee Wee would love your roast chicken."

"And maybe he'd like some salad, too."

"Salad would be good," said Harry. "And chocolate cupcakes." Harry thought for a moment. "Do you feel better now, Mom?" he said.

"I feel much better," said his mother.

Mr. Kane was wrapping glasses now. "Joshua's mother said she'll really miss Harry. She said he has a great personality."

"Do I?" said Harry.

"You do," said his mother.

Harry was quiet. Finally he said, "What's a personality?"

Mrs. Kane thought. "Well," she said. "A personality is . . . the things about a person that make him unique."

"What's unique?" said Harry.

Mr. Kane took a plastic bunny cup with a crack in it and put it in the garbage can. "Unique is . . . what makes you special."

"Oh," said Harry. "I see." Harry walked over to the garbage can and picked up the lid. He reached in and pulled out the cracked bunny cup. "I'll need this," he said to his father.

"Why?" said Mr. Kane. "It has a crack in it."

Harry took a piece of newspaper and wrapped it around his cup. "For the new house," he said. "To remember when I was little."

Harry's mother rubbed his head. "Harry," she said, "you're really something."

Harry smiled. "And I have a great personality, too."

The door slammed, and Chloe and Dorothy came into the kitchen.

"What's for supper?" said Chloe, putting her library books on the kitchen table.

"I'm starving!" said Dorothy.

"Me, too!" said Harry.

Mrs. Kane looked at Mr. Kane. "What do you think?" she said, holding up a piece of newspaper. "Newspaper casserole?"

"Ugh!" said Chloe.

"Yuck!" said Dorothy.

"Pizza!" said Harry, jumping up and down. "Pizza, pizza, pizza."

Mrs. Kane picked up Chloe's books and handed them to her. "In your room, please, and then we can go for pizza."

"Why?" said Chloe. "We don't need the table. We're eating out."

"Because I'll pack them," said Mrs. Kane, "and you'll never see them again."

Harry followed Chloe to her room. "I have an idea," he said.

"What?" said Chloe, combing her hair.

Harry wondered why girls were always combing their hair. But instead of asking, he said, "Let's go to the pizza store by the pet shop."

"Why?" said Chloe, fixing a bow in her hair.

"Because I like pet shops," said Harry.

Dorothy appeared in the doorway. "What about a pet shop?" she said.

Harry smiled. "I think our new house needs a pet!" he said. "That way Mom and I won't be so lonely."

"Harry!" said Chloe, putting her hands on her hips. "For a little kid, you have great ideas!"

"I know," said Harry, putting his hands in his pockets. "And I have a great personality, too."

At the restaurant, the waitress brought a whole pizza to the table, and Mrs. Kane gave each of them a slice. "Mushroom for you and Chloe," she said to Harry. "And plain for the rest of us."

Harry was so excited about the pet shop that he could hardly eat his pizza. He thought he could hear barking and meowing and squawking through the wall. He wondered if a puppy would like mushroom pizza as much as he did.

"Dad," said Harry, popping a mushroom into his mouth. "Didn't you have a dog when you were little?"

"I certainly did," said Mr. Kane. "His name was Buster."

"It must have been great," said Chloe, wondering if a dog would eat leftover pizza crust.

"It was for a while," said Mr. Kane. "But we had to give him away. Don't you remember? I'm allergic to dogs."

"Oh," said Chloe glumly. "I forgot." Chloe could see that dogs were out.

It was Dorothy's turn. "Mom," said Dorothy brightly. "Didn't you have a cat when you were little?"

"I did," said Mrs. Kane, sipping her soda. "Until the cat started scratching all of my mother's good furniture."

"Oh," said Dorothy. Dorothy could see that cats were out.

Mr. Kane spoke up. "But my mother got me some fish. Some pretty goldfish in a little bowl, to cheer me up when she gave Buster away."

"Fish?" said Harry. Fish were boring. But dogs were out, and so were cats. Harry could see that. "Joshua's hamster Pee Wee is the greatest," he said.

Mr. Kane sniffed. "I know you like him, Harry. But to tell you the truth, hamsters remind me of rats. And I couldn't ever see myself living with a rat."

Harry could see that hamsters were out.

They finished their pizza and left the restaurant. Chloe pressed her nose against the windowpane of the pet shop. "Harry!" said Chloe. "Look!"

Harry stood next to Chloe and pressed his nose against the glass. "Birds!" he whispered to Chloe. Maybe they could try for a bird.

"A yellow bird," said Chloe.

"A bird that talks," said Dorothy, pressing her nose next to Harry's.

"A yellow bird that talks!" said Harry.

Mrs. Kane folded her arms together. "Now I see where all of this talk has been leading to," she said to Mr. Kane.

"No birds," said Mr. Kane firmly. "I don't want a bird landing on my head in my new house."

Harry could see that birds were out. But Harry wouldn't give up. "Can we go inside, anyway?" he said.

"Just for a minute," said Mr. Kane, opening the door. They could hear all sorts of noises—squawking and barking and squealing and squeaking. But birds and cats and hamsters and dogs were out, and fish were boring.

Harry headed past the brightly colored fish in the aquariums. He glanced quickly at the puppies gnawing rubber bones in their cages. He waved to the marmalade cat meowing in another cage. A green parrot flapped its wings and said, "Hello, hello!"

"Good-bye," said Harry, because Harry had a purpose. He searched the store until he found what he was looking for. He stood in front of a giant plastic swimming pool, like the one by his grandma's hotel when she went to Florida. It even had plastic palm trees.

"A turtle," he whispered, watching them crawl around in their swimming pool home. One green and black turtle, about four inches long, scurried quickly toward Harry. He pressed his head against the plastic. He peered at Harry.

Harry knew what he had to do. He found his father and took his hand. "When we move away," he said to his father, "I won't be lonely if I share my room with him."

"With whom?" said Mr. Kane, letting Harry lead him to the back of the store.

"With him," said Harry, showing his father the green and black turtle, who was waiting for Harry. "He's faster than the rest," Harry added.

"I see," said Mr. Kane.

"I can sing to him at night, instead of to Dorothy," said Harry.

"I see," said Mr. Kane. "And will you feed him every day?"

"Yes," said Harry. "And he'll keep me from getting scared."

"I see," said Mr. Kane. "And will you keep his bowl clean?"

"Yes," said Harry, watching his turtle scurry back and forth in front of him. "And he won't make you allergic, and he won't scratch Mom's furniture, and he won't land on your head, and he doesn't look like a rat."

"That's true," said his father.

Mr. Kane went and found Mrs. Kane, and Harry watched him whisper something in her ear. Then Mrs. Kane went over to the big counter with the cash register and spoke to the man behind it.

The man locked his cash register and came over to Harry.

"Which one will it be?" said the man, holding his hand out over the swimming pool home with the plastic palm trees.

"That one," said Harry, pointing to the green and black turtle. "The one with personality."

And that's how Harry got his pet turtle. And that's how Harry named him Personality.

3

First Day

WHEN HARRY FOUND OUT that his mother couldn't take him to school on his very first day of kindergarten, Harry cried.

"I'm so sorry, Harry," said his mother, dabbing his eyes with a tissue. "It's Grandma. Grandpa Leon called, and he's very worried about her. She won't go to the doctor's."

Harry blew his nose in the tissue his mother was holding. "I don't like going to the doctor's, either," he said, sniffling. "Maybe she's afraid he'll give her a shot."

"Maybe," said his mother. "I'm just going to drive over there tonight and take her to the doctor's tomorrow."

Chloe looked up from the game of Chutes and Ladders she was playing with Dorothy. "I can take Harry to school," she said. "I'll be in the third grade."

"So can I," said Dorothy. "We can take care of Harry together."

Chloe gave Dorothy an icy look. "You can't even compare the third grade with the second grade. You and Harry are just babies."

Harry's mother held up her hands like a stop sign. "It's all arranged," she said. "Mrs. Peet next door is going to take you to school with her daughter Natasha. Natasha's going into the first grade."

"Big deal," said Chloe. "I'm still the oldest."

Harry had other ideas. "I've decided to stay home and keep Personality company," said Harry. "He hasn't been eating his lettuce ever since we

27

moved here. I can show him books about turtles. We can make drawings of turtles. And you can take me to school the next day."

"I don't think so, Harry," said his mother softly. "But I do have a surprise for you." She reached into her pocketbook and handed Harry a tiny brown paper package.

"For me?" said Harry, squeezing it in his hands. He opened it up. It was a fuzzy little red bear, with a pin on the back of it.

"A bear?" said Harry. Harry screwed up his nose. He turned the bear over and examined the pin. "A bear pin? Pins are for girls."

"I'll take it!" said Chloe. "It's cute!"

"It'll match my new red school outfit," said Dorothy.

"I'm wearing it," said Mrs. Kane. She took the pin from Harry and fastened it to her shirt.

"Then why did you say it was for me?" said Harry.

"Because I'll wear it all day today, until I leave for Grandma's. And tomorrow you'll wear it on your knapsack when you go to kindergarten. That way, part of me will be with you."

Harry looked at the bear pinned to his mother's collar. "I guess he's kind of cute," said Harry. "But I have a better idea. Why don't I bring Personality with me, to keep the bear company?"

Chloe rolled her eyes. "Sure, Harry. Your teacher would love it. I can just see her screaming when she finds Personality crawling across her desk."

Harry was annoyed. "What good is a kindergarten teacher who doesn't like turtles?" he said.

Harry's mother laughed. "I'm sure she likes turtles," she said. "Who knows, Harry? Maybe you'll like your kindergarten teacher as much as you like Personality!"

"I doubt it," said Harry. "I'm going to get ready for school now."

Harry went to his bedroom closet and got out a brand-new pair of white sneakers with rainbow laces and laid them on the bed. Then he took out of his dresser a clean red button-down shirt and a new pair of jeans with the tags still on them. He put them next to his sneakers. Then he went to his desk and found his plastic Batman pencil case with five sharpened pencils in it, an eraser, and a felt-tip pen. He put the pencil case next to his shirt.

His mother poked her head in the door. "All set?" she said.

"Almost," said Harry, rummaging in the bottom of his closet.

"You have to sleep on that bed tonight," said his mother.

Harry shrugged his shoulders. "I can always sleep next to Personality on the floor," he said.

"I'll come kiss you good-bye before I leave," said Mrs. Kane.

"Okay," said Harry. Then he pulled out his bright blue knapsack, with the brontosaurus on it, and laid it next to his pencil case. "A little bear is going to keep you company," he said to the brontosaurus. Then he left the bedroom and closed the door. "I'm ready!" he called to his mother.

Harry didn't like being new, especially on the first day of school. He woke up in his new house, put on his new clothes, and walked slowly down his new street with his new neighbors Mrs. Peet and Natasha. Natasha was skipping ahead excitedly, but she was with her mother, and she wasn't new.

"Could you move a little faster, Harry?" said Mrs. Peet in the nicest possible voice. Harry knew that she could have said, "Stop dragging your feet, Harry," instead. Chloe was moving only a tiny bit faster than Harry, tying and retying a big yellow bow at the back of her hair, and Dorothy was picking at her fingernails even while she walked. Harry suspected that maybe Chloe and Dorothy didn't like being new, either.

Walnut School was only a block away from the house. Harry could hear the children shouting and laughing in the playground outside the school. They sounded happy, too, but of course they weren't new, and they didn't have to come to school with a new neighbor down a new street, without their mothers.

They reached the schoolyard.

"Here we are!" sang Mrs. Peet as they entered.

"Goody, goody," mumbled Chloe, and she pulled out a slip of paper her mother had given her. "I have the room numbers," said Chloe. "My mother said I should take care of Harry and Dorothy."

"Oh," said Mrs. Peet, looking confused. "Well, I'll just walk you inside the school."

Dorothy poked Chloe in the arm. "Mom never said any such thing," she hissed.

"So?" said Chloe. "Would you rather let everybody see you with some woman who isn't even your mother?"

"I'll go with you," said Harry, and he took Chloe's hand.

They left Mrs. Peet in the hallway. "Here's Natasha's room," she called out to them, but Chloe just waved. "I'll pick you up after school," Mrs. Peet called louder.

Chloe consulted her piece of paper and turned down another hallway. "Room two for Harry," she said out loud. "And Dorothy, you're room eleven."

"Harry's right here!" said Dorothy excitedly. "Room two-K. K must be for kindergarten." Dorothy felt very grown-up, finding Harry's room for him.

"And here's room eleven!" called Chloe from down the hall.

A bell rang loudly, and Harry held his ears. "You go," Dorothy called back to Chloe. "I'll take Harry in."

Dorothy took Harry's hand, and they entered the classroom.

"Look at this," whispered Dorothy to Harry. "You get your own desk. I never had my own desk when I went to kindergarten."

Harry sat down. He put his knapsack under his desk. "You can go now," he said to Dorothy in a small voice.

"Don't be afraid," said Dorothy, giving him a good-bye hug. "I'm just next door in room eleven."

A teacher stood in front of the room and wrote something on the blackboard. It was the first big blackboard Harry had ever seen.

"My name is Mrs. Singer," said the lady.

"And she can't even sing," said somebody behind Harry.

Mrs. Singer called out the children's names from a piece of paper. "Applegate. Bell. Carpenter. Cohen."

After each name was called, someone would raise a hand and say, "Here!" To Harry, it sounded as if she was reading from some weird kind of alphabet book. She continued straight through to Z for Zimmerman.

Mrs. Singer put the list on her desk. "Was anyone's name not called?"

Harry looked around. He was afraid to raise his hand. He was afraid to open his mouth.

"The little guy," said a voice behind him. "In the red shirt."

"What's your name?" said Mrs. Singer, looking down her nose at Harry.

"Harry," said Harry.

"He must be new," said the voice behind him.

"I'm new," said Harry in a tiny voice.

Mrs. Singer wrote something on a piece of paper. "Matthew," she said. "Will you take this to Mr. Torres's office?"

Matthew took the piece of paper, and Mrs. Singer continued. "Now open up your readers to page one. Let's see how much reading you got done this summer."

Harry peered into the cubbyhole under his desk just as the other children were doing. He looked at the three books sitting inside his desk. One, two, three. He could count to three. He could even count to twenty. But he couldn't read.

"Sophie," said Mrs. Singer. "Would you like to start?"

Harry picked up his knapsack. He took out his Batman pencil case and put it on his desk. Then he opened up the knapsack as wide as he could make it, and he put it on his head. He laid his head on the desk. It was dark inside the knapsack. It was safe. Harry started to cry, without making any noise. He wondered how many tears it would take to fill up the knapsack. He was glad Personality

wasn't there with him. Personality would have
been sad, too. Personality couldn't read, either. He
wished he was home with Personality eating lettuce
and chopped meat from the refrigerator. Kindergarten was terrible. And Mrs. Singer looked like
someone who hated turtles.

"Harry." His name was being called, but Harry
stayed where he was. "Harry!" The voice was
louder. He could feel his face getting hot inside the
knapsack. Now there was another voice. "Harry?"
It was a man's voice. Little beads of sweat broke
out on Harry's forehead, and he couldn't tell if it
was tears or sweat trickling down his cheek.
"Harry Kane?" said the voice sternly.

"What?" said Harry, hiccuping, so that it
sounded like "Wha-hup," from under the knapsack.

"Come with me, Harry," said the man's voice,
and a hand touched his shoulder.

Harry pulled the knapsack off his head. He took
the man's hand. He passed Mrs. Singer, who he
was sure hated turtles, and he didn't even look at

her. His mother would be upset with him for messing up his first day of kindergarten. It was worse than feeding one of her supper hamburgers to Personality. Much worse.

It was cooler in the hallway. "I think you were in the wrong classroom," said the man, who wore brown glasses like his father's. "You were in the second grade."

"I'm supposed to be in kindergarten," said Harry, his voice a little wobbly. "My sister Dorothy is in eleven."

"Eleven?" said the man. "We don't have the eleventh grade here, so maybe you mean room eleven, where the other second grade class is." The man with Harry's father's glasses took Harry's hand again. "Let's go see."

Dorothy looked startled when a strange man in a suit appeared in the doorway of her new classroom holding her little brother's hand. Maybe he wet his pants, she thought. Maybe the man wants me to clean him up.

"Dorothy Kane?" said the man. "Is that your sister?" he said to Harry as Dorothy stood up.

"Yes," whispered Harry.

"I'm afraid your brother has had a difficult morning," said the man to Dorothy. "I'm the principal, Mr. Torres. Do you happen to know why your brother was put in the second grade instead of kindergarten?"

Dorothy could hear children laughing behind her. She said in the tiniest voice she could make, "I did it." The laughter sounded louder, and she could feel her face turn very red.

"It's okay," said Harry. He thought his sister Dorothy was going to cry.

"Let me show you where I'm putting your brother," said the principal. He led them both along the hallway and down a flight of stairs. Harry thought maybe it was a dungeon for dumb children who couldn't read, with bats and rats and black hairy spiders. Their feet pattered loudly in the stairwell.

"Here we are," said the principal, and Harry's

heart started to hammer. He hoped they didn't have to read right away in this room.

"It's pretty," whispered Dorothy. Her face wasn't as red now.

Harry looked at the brightly colored flowers hanging on the walls. The teacher came over, and she was wearing a green dress, with red lipstick on her mouth the same as his mother wore. Harry thought green was a nice color. Personality was the same color.

"You must be Harry," said the teacher, and she bent down and looked straight into his eyes. "We thought we'd lost you, Harry," said the teacher. "I'm Mrs. Moss."

Moss was good. Turtles like moss. Harry looked around. Some of the children were coloring on large pieces of construction paper. Others were building a fort out of blocks.

Harry turned to Dorothy. "You can go now," said Harry.

"Are you sure?" said Dorothy.

"I'm sure," said Harry. "I can do all this," he added, waving his arm around the room.

"Here's your knapsack," said the principal, and Mrs. Moss showed Harry where his cubbyhole would be. Harry set the knapsack in his new cubbyhole with his name above it. Soon he would be able to read more than his name. For now, Harry unpinned the little bear from his knapsack and pinned it on his sleeve. It didn't look too sissy. Anyway, Harry didn't really care if it did. It was time to build a fort.

4

Harry and the Birds

FOR HARRY, going to assembly was an adventure, especially when his teacher, Mrs. Moss, kept the program a secret. Harry followed his new friend Benjamin into the auditorium. On the first day of school, Harry and Benjamin had become friends by building a Batman fort together, and outsmarting the Joker, who was really a boy named Joe who pushed and shoved a lot. Benjamin was even funnier than Harry's old friend Joshua, but he didn't have a pet hamster named Pee Wee.

They took their seats and watched Mrs. Moss,

who put her finger to her mouth, telling them to quiet down. The lights dimmed, and Harry felt excited.

There was a man on the stage, with longish hair and a mustache. Mr. Torres, the principal, stepped up onto the stage next to him and said, "Today, we have a very special treat in store for you. This is Mr. Olinder, and he is a licensed falconer."

A falconer was someone who trained and bred falcons, Mr. Torres explained, but Harry hardly listened. He was busy craning his neck to look at the different-size boxes on a long table that looked as if it came from the cafeteria. Mr. Olinder stepped forward. He was wearing a T-shirt and jeans, not a suit like Mr. Torres. He told them all about his rehabilitation center for injured birds, and how he tried to retrain them to go back into the wild and learn to hunt again.

Then Mr. Olinder put on a leather glove and reached behind a cloth-covered box. There was a flapping sound, and Mr. Olinder pulled out his first guest.

"This is Beauty," said Mr. Olinder, "and he is a peregrine falcon. He measures about eighteen inches, and he dives on his prey from the air, sometimes as fast as one hundred seventy-five miles per hour. That's three times as fast as your parents' car on the highway. He eats mostly birds, like pigeons and crows."

Beauty flapped his wings, and Harry saw something splatter onto the newspaper covering the floor. Mr. Olinder didn't seem to mind that Beauty wasn't toilet trained, because he kept on talking.

"We found Beauty by the side of a road, with an injured eye where a bullet had grazed him. Beauty can never go back into the wild, because his eye waters a lot. And whenever it does, he wipes at it with his wing. So now there are no feathers under his eye, and if he was left in the wild, his face would freeze and he would die."

Harry kept his eyes glued to Beauty. He remembered that once, Mr. Simpkins, the custodian, found a pigeon in the auditorium and had a lot of trouble getting it out the window. Harry pulled up his feet in case the falcon smelled pigeon on the floor and decided to get it for his lunch. He was glad that he had decided not to bring Personality to school today. Personality would have made a delicious snack for Beauty, if he couldn't find a pigeon.

Mr. Olinder's next guest was an owl named Hooter. He was called a barred owl, because of the barlike stripes across his chest. He had beautiful eyes, almost the size of a human's, and, like Beauty, he turned his head every which way. It looked as if Hooter could turn his head all the way around, if he wanted to.

Hooter wasn't as scary as Beauty, but Harry was a little disappointed. It turned out that owls weren't wise at all—they were not half as smart as falcons or eagles. They just looked smart. And they ate little mice and even small birds, like the sparrows that hopped on Harry's father's bird feeder. But Hooter had a pretty face, and he seemed to like Mr. Olinder a lot.

After Mr. Olinder put Hooter away, he held up his hands. He looked very serious, like Harry's mother when she found Harry carrying Personality around in her best mixing bowl.

"I need your cooperation now," said Mr. Olinder. "I'd like you to meet my newest and largest guest. It has been a rare privilege to work with him. He is our national bird."

There were whispers throughout the auditorium, and Mr. Olinder held up his hands again. "I'll get him out, but I warn you. If I don't have absolute quiet, I won't be able to get him back in. If King decides he doesn't want to return to his cage, all he has to do is hold out one wing. He's in charge."

Harry held his breath. Benjamin gripped Harry's knee with his hand. There was a long "Oooohhh" as Mr. Olinder took out a giant bald eagle with powerful talons. Harry noticed that the eagle wasn't bald at all—he had a white feathered head. King didn't look too happy sitting on Mr. Olinder's hand, because Mr. Olinder couldn't hold it steady, and his arm kept drooping. Harry thought maybe he should tell Mr. Olinder to start lifting weights like his father.

Suddenly, King flapped up into the air, and the newspapers on the floor flew across the stage. Harry put his hand to his mouth. Mr. Olinder pulled on a thin rope and cupped his hand around King's chest, and King settled down again. Mr. Olinder said that King was the smartest of them all—he was also a powerful flier, with the keenest eyesight, and he could pluck chickens, skin rabbits, and take the heads off fish. He sounded a little like Harry's mother's butcher, who really *was* bald.

Mr. Olinder put his finger to his lips, just as Mrs. Moss had done. He moved behind King's cage and bent down. There was a great flapping sound, and Harry could see a wing rise into the air. A woman in the audience that Harry had never seen before half rose from her seat. The cage clanged shut, and the woman sat down again. Harry sighed with relief, and so did Benjamin. King was back in his cage.

Mr. Olinder asked if they had any questions.

Lots of hands shot into the air. One little girl asked why the birds were so mean, eating all those little animals.

"They eat to survive," said Mr. Olinder. "Hooter can kill a mouse in less than twenty seconds. Your cat can take twenty minutes playing with it and throwing it against the wall. I'd rather be killed by an owl than a cat."

Harry thought he'd rather not be killed at all. He'd rather play cops and robbers with Benjamin, or Chutes and Ladders with his sister Dorothy.

Harry raised his hand. "Did you ever get hurt by one of your birds?" he said.

Mr. Olinder nodded his head. "One day, I wasn't paying attention to Beauty, and Beauty decided that he wanted to play with my shirt. He hooked his talons right through my shirt and into my chest. The more I tried to pull him away, the harder he held on. It was like getting caught by a large fish hook."

Everybody made noises that sounded like "Ugh" and "Yick," and Harry raised his hand again.

"How did you get away?" he asked.

"I screamed for my wife," said Mr. Olinder, "and she came running in with one of these." He

47

held up a little leather hood. "Lena, stand up and take a bow," said Mr. Olinder, pointing with the hood toward the strange woman in the audience. "Lena rushed in and slipped one of these over Beauty's head, and Beauty quieted right down and removed his claws."

Harry whispered into Benjamin's ear, "Ask him to show us the scar!" Harry knew that Benjamin liked scars as much as he did, because just that morning, Benjamin had shown him a really great one on his left elbow.

But Benjamin shook his head, and Harry said a little louder, "Go ahead. Ask him!" There was a shushing sound from behind Harry that came from a teacher, and both of them crunched down in their seats until the question-and-answer period was over.

After the presentation, Harry's class returned to their classroom. They drew pictures of their favorite birds. Harry painted the bald eagle, even though he ate a lot of little animals the size of Personality, or even bigger.

□   □   □

Mrs. Kane met Harry and Dorothy and Chloe outside the school, and all they could talk about was Mr. Olinder's birds.

"The bald eagle doesn't have babies until he's five years old, like me," said Harry.

Mrs. Kane laughed and said that children had to wait a lot longer than eagles before they were grown-up.

"Five is grown-up," Harry insisted, but he didn't argue.

"Owls aren't really wise," said Dorothy as she took her mother's hand. "Mr. Olinder says that's only a potato chip advertisement, and their brain is smaller than a golf ball."

Mrs. Kane laughed again. "You certainly learned a lot today," she said. "How about you, Chloe? Which was your favorite?"

Chloe didn't hesitate. "Beauty, the falcon. But I felt sorry for his eye."

When they got home, Harry wouldn't play Mommy and Daddy with Dorothy and Chloe.

Sometimes, if he was in a good mood, he would be the baby, but only if he could be a bad baby, or a messy baby. Today, Harry had other ideas.

"I'll be the owl," said Harry, "and you two will be the mice."

Dorothy and Chloe crawled around on the floor. It was hard to run quickly on all fours like a fast mouse would do. They sat and cleaned their whiskers, and suddenly Harry swooped down from the couch on top of them, shouting "Gotcha!" Dorothy and Chloe screamed, and Mrs. Kane came running into the living room. She didn't like the game very much and tried to get them to eat a snack of sliced apples.

This time, Chloe and Harry nibbled on apples, and Dorothy swooped down like a giant bald eagle would, yelling "Gotcha!" Then she made believe she was crunching and munching on Harry's ear and Chloe's cheeks until they screamed so much that Mrs. Kane made them go upstairs and play in their rooms.

Chloe and Dorothy decided to dress up like princesses, but Harry didn't want to be the prince. He knew they would make him wear the pink plastic tiara with the diamonds on it, and it hurt his ears.

Harry went into his bedroom and walked straight over to Personality, who was sitting on a rock in his plastic swimming pool, with his head inside his shell. As soon as he heard Harry's voice, he poked his head out.

"You were lucky you didn't go to school today," said Harry, petting Personality's shell. "I saw lots of birds today that would have liked you for their lunch."

Personality jumped into the water and took a swim. Harry knew exactly what that meant, in turtle language. Personality was happy that he was living with Harry in his new house. And Personality was even happier that he hadn't been eaten by a giant bald eagle for lunch.

5

Personality's Final Adventure

PERSONALITY WASN'T LIKE any ordinary turtle. He was an explorer. He liked to walk across the ledge of the Kanes' shiny new bathtub. He liked to crawl up Harry's blue jeans to the top of Harry's knee. Harry was sure that Personality thought he was climbing a mountain.

"He likes adventure," said Dorothy, watching Personality explore Harry's potted plant.

"He thinks he's hiking," explained Harry. "He takes after me."

"A turtle can't take after a little boy," said Chloe.

"Personality can," answered Harry.

One day after school, Harry said good-bye to Natasha Peet at the door. He said hello to his mother in the kitchen. Then he opened up the refrigerator door and plucked a few pieces of lettuce from the salad drawer. He took an apple for himself and went upstairs to visit Personality.

Harry ran to his desk and dangled a piece of lettuce over Personality's plastic swimming pool. He looked inside. The rock was there. The colored pebbles were there. The plastic seaweed was there. But Personality was gone.

It took a long time to calm Harry down.

"Maybe he's gone on another adventure," said Dorothy, trying to cheer Harry up. She missed Personality, too. Sometimes Harry let Personality climb to the top of Dorothy's knee, as if it were a mountain.

"He wouldn't go without me," said Harry, a tear rolling down his cheek.

Chloe started a search party. She assigned each

one of them a room, and they set to work. They looked inside wastepaper baskets, under beds, on windowsills, inside boxes of blocks, in Dorothy's pink baby carriage, in closets, in the bathtub, and even in the soap dish. Personality was nowhere to be found.

Suppertime came, and Harry hardly ate a thing. Chloe told him he should keep up his strength, because they would search some more after supper. Harry cried when Mr. Kane gave him a bowl of salad. "That's Personality's dinner," he sobbed, and he pushed the bowl away so that a tomato rolled out of the bowl and across the table. Mr. Kane didn't even get mad. "I'll help you look after supper," he said.

Dorothy watched carefully where she was walking as she started searching again. She knew she would feel even worse if she stepped on poor Personality by mistake and squashed him.

"He's taking a trip," she whispered to Harry before he got into bed. She looked under Harry's covers, just in case.

Harry was sad for at least a week. Harry's mother made him his favorite meals so that he would start eating again. At school, Dorothy painted a picture of Personality. She hung it on Harry's wall, and her mother didn't even say anything about the marks it would make on the paint.

One day, Dorothy and Chloe were playing Mommy and Daddy. Harry lay in bed and was even a good baby. Dorothy couldn't get used to it. "Can't you cry?" she said to Harry. Chloe gave Harry a toy bottle, and he held it in his hands instead of throwing it away, the way he used to do.

"I liked it better when Harry was a bad baby," whispered Chloe.

"Me, too," whispered Dorothy back. Harry just wasn't the same without Personality.

Soon it was time for the mommy and daddy to get ready for bed, so Dorothy went into her parents' bedroom closet to get her parents' old slippers. She gave her father's beat-up moccasins that he never wore anymore to Chloe, and she kept her mother's bunny slippers for herself. Her mother said they made her feet sweat, so she let Dorothy play with them.

Only this time, when Dorothy put one of her bare feet into her mother's pink bunny slipper, it wouldn't go all the way in. She wiggled her toes. Something wiggled back.

Dorothy's screams brought her mother running into the room. By this time, Dorothy was on the bed, and she pointed to the pink bunny slipper on the floor.

"Something's inside it," she whispered. "Maybe it's a mouse, or a huge spider!"

Mrs. Kane didn't look anxious to put her hand inside the slipper, but before she could stop him, Harry put his whole fist inside.

And out came Personality, safe and sound and very much alive.

The whole family gave Personality a homecoming party. Harry had never looked so happy. He looked happier than when his father let him ride three times on the Ferris wheel at the amusement park. He looked happier than when he ate a large bowl of his favorite ice cream, vanilla fudge. He smiled the whole time that he fed Personality some lettuce. He even let Dorothy feed him some chopped meat. While the family ate hamburgers, Mrs. Kane let Personality sit in a bowl on a chair and eat his dinner. She made Harry wash his hands before he ate his own.

"I can't believe I'm eating dinner with a turtle," said Harry's father.

After supper, Mr. Kane cut a piece of wire mesh to fit over the top of Personality's plastic swimming pool. Harry put his Batman figure on top of the wire netting so that Personality wouldn't push aside the netting and go off on another adventure. He went to bed that night with a smile on his face, listening to Personality thump happily about in his swimming pool. It was nice having Personality back in the family again.

But Personality didn't stay for long. Two days later, he was gone again. Mr. Kane said Personality had adventure in the blood. Dorothy made another picture of Personality, even better than the first one, but Harry wouldn't put it up on the wall. Mrs. Kane found his book about turtles in the wastepaper basket. And Harry wouldn't wear the color green anymore.

The next time Dorothy and Chloe played Mommy and Daddy, Harry played the bad baby. He was the worst baby in the world. He threw his bottle against the wall, so that it left a scratch. He screamed and pounded pillows. He punched Dorothy's best baby doll on the head.

"You're a terrible baby," Dorothy told him as he spit a Cheerio at her. "I don't want to play with you anymore."

"Who cares?" said Harry, and he lay across his bed with his hand on top of the wire netting across the empty plastic swimming pool.

Harry heard a scream coming from the direction of the laundry room. His mother had never screamed like that before, and it scared him. Harry and Dorothy and Chloe ran to the laundry room and stopped still in their tracks, like statues. Mrs. Kane had a terrible look on her face, as if Harry had thrown up in her lap or something. She pointed to the table. Next to a pile of folded towels was a shriveled-up green shell that looked a little like Personality.

"He went through the washer and dryer," she whispered.

Harry looked at the green shell. He looked at the spinning dryer. "It's not him," he whispered.

Dorothy looked at the dryer, too. She could see socks and sheets and even one of Harry's stuffed bears going around and around in the machine. "Maybe," she whispered, "it felt like a ride on the Ferris wheel. You love the Ferris wheel, Harry."

"I don't think so," said Harry. He took his favorite Sesame Street washcloth off the pile of folded towels and picked up the green shell. Then he wrapped the washcloth around Personality.

"I'd like a pretty box," he said to his mother. "For the funeral."

Mrs. Kane went upstairs and took her shell

59

necklace out of its silver box. She gave the box to Harry. Dorothy helped Harry tape up the box, with the washcloth and Personality inside, because the cover kept popping off. Chloe wrote a poem for the funeral.

They dug a hole in the backyard next to a holly bush with red berries on it.

"Personality liked bright colors," said Harry.

Chloe read her poem out loud.

> "Personality was our turtle.
> We got him for our new house.
> He was better than a goldfish
> And much better than a mouse.
> We'll miss him very deeply.
> We're sad he went away.
> But now we have our memories
> Of a turtle who couldn't stay."

Harry put Personality in the ground and covered the box with dirt. Then, taking turns, first Harry, then Dorothy, and then Chloe stomped on the dirt so that it was flat and smooth.

Harry picked a few red berries and pressed them into the ground.

"He's at peace now," said Chloe.

"Good-bye, Personality," said Dorothy.

They went inside the house. Mrs. Kane was on the telephone with Grandma. Harry tapped his mother.

"I want to talk to Grandma," he said.

"Hold on, Mother. Harry wants to talk to you," said Mrs. Kane. She handed the phone to Harry.

"Grandma?" said Harry. "Personality died."

"I'm so sorry, darling," said Grandma. "You must be upset."

"I'm very sad," said Harry. "He was my friend. But he liked adventure."

"Was he sick?" said Grandma.

Harry paused for a moment. It was too awful, the idea of Personality going around and around in a washer and dryer. At last, he said, "He was carried away by a giant bald eagle. It was his final adventure. I have to go now, Grandma."

"Good-bye, darling," said Grandma.

"Good-bye, Grandma," said Harry, and he handed the phone to his mother.

Harry went upstairs to his room. He took Dorothy's picture of Personality and put it up on his wall, right next to his painting of King, the giant bald eagle. Then he took the rock that Personality liked to sit on, and he stuck it in the pot with his flowering cactus. He put the cactus pot on his desk, in front of the picture of Personality.

"Good-bye, Personality," he said, touching the rock. "I'll miss you."

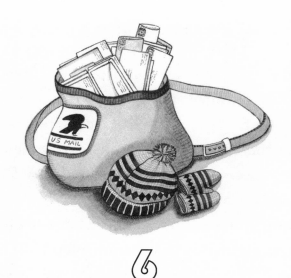

6

Harry's Career

WHEN HARRY was little and Grandma asked him what he wanted to be when he grew up, Harry answered, "An ice-cream cone."

"But you'll get eaten up," said Grandma, laughing.

"Then I'll be a man who sells ice cream," said Harry. After all, ice cream was his favorite food in the whole world.

"You eat so much ice cream, you'll turn into an ice-cream cone," said his sister Chloe.

"You'll turn into an Oreo cookie," said Harry. Harry had an answer for everything.

Now that Harry was five years old, when his grandmother asked him what he wanted to be when he grew up, Harry answered, "A letter carrier, just like my daddy."

Grandma smiled and said, "That's a fine job."

One day, Harry's father took Harry with him to the post office. They got up at five-thirty in the morning and had breakfast.

"Get something hot down you, Harry," said Mr. Kane. "It's a long day, and it's cold out there."

Harry turned up his nose at the hot cereal, but it tasted better with lots of brown sugar and butter and raisins and milk.

It was dark outside when they left the house.

"Smells like snow," said Harry's father.

Harry sniffed. The air was so cold that his nose felt like an ice cube. The streets were empty except for old Mr. Lester, who was walking his even older bulldog.

"Her plumbing isn't what it used to be," said Mr. Lester, shaking his head.

"I'm going to work with my father," said Harry proudly.

"Are you, now?" said Mr. Lester, his breath coming out in great puffs. "I'll expect my mail on time, then!" he said as the old bulldog pulled him away.

Inside the post office, Harry couldn't believe the hustle and bustle and the bright lights. Harry's father handed him his time card and let Harry punch it into the time clock.

There were stacks of mail on what Mr. Kane called pie carts.

"Where are the pies?" said Harry.

"No pies," said Mr. Kane. "The clerk distributes the mail to my desk. Here we are, desk number sixteen."

Four trays of mail sat on Mr. Kane's desk, and Mr. Kane began rapidly sorting the envelopes into pigeonholes with street numbers under them.

"I do the first-class mail first," said Mr. Kane.

"The important mail," said Harry.

"Then I get my packages and parcels under two

65

pounds," said Mr. Kane. He showed Harry where to stack them.

"Then I empty my bag of flats," said Mr. Kane, "my magazines, newspapers, and catalogs, and I put them off to the side."

"That's the second-class mail," said Harry.

"Correct," said Mr. Kane, handing an empty tray to the clerk. "And what do you think this is?" he said, holding up a bunch of advertisements and letters marked bulk rate.

"Third class!" said Harry proudly.

At last, Mr. Kane pulled the first-class letters out of their slots and carefully placed the stacks into a mailbag. Then he gave the sacks to the man loading the trucks.

"He'll take them to the storage boxes, and then my real work can begin," said Mr. Kane.

Harry thought that three hours of sorting mail was enough work. He was tired. But he perked up when his father brought over a plate of chocolate chip cookies, a thermos cup of milk, and a container of coffee.

"Coffee break," said Mr. Kane, handing Harry his cup. Harry blew on his milk as if it was hot coffee. He felt very grown-up, drinking coffee with all the letter carriers.

"Drink up," said Harry's father, putting on his jacket. "It's time to deliver the mail."

Harry and his father drove to Elm Street. Mr. Kane unlocked the storage box and unloaded the mail into his satchel. They started walking.

"It's cold out," said Harry, shivering.

"It's invigorating," said Mr. Kane, pulling Harry's woolen cap down around his ears. "Think warm thoughts," he said.

Harry thought about a cup of hot chocolate, but he still felt goose bumps on his arms.

They opened a gate and walked down a path to a rickety porch.

"Watch your step," said Mr. Kane as Harry's foot nearly went through a hole in the wooden step. "Number eighteen," he said, depositing the mail into the metal box.

The next house was in better shape, but when

they got to the front door, Harry heard a deep growl. A dog much bigger than Mr. Lester's old bulldog rounded the corner at a gallop, and Harry thought his heart would stop.

"Forgot to warn you," said Mr. Kane. "But don't worry. He's tied up."

The dog was straining against the rope, which was attached to a clothesline on a runner so that the dog could run back and forth.

"Does he bite?" said Harry, not reaching out to pet him the way he would normally do. "Nice doggie," he added. The dog bared his yellow teeth again, and Harry thought he saw bits of foam coming out of his mouth.

"Maybe he has rabies," said Harry to his father.

"The owner says he's harmless," said Mr. Kane. "But I never believe them."

They left number twenty and turned toward number twenty-two.

An old lady met them at the door. Harry brightened. Maybe she had a cup of hot chocolate for them.

The lady stuck a wrinkled hand with blue veins all over it out of the door. "A book of stamps," she said.

Mr. Kane pulled off his glove and reached into his pocket. "Here you are, Mrs. Arnold," he said as he handed her the stamps and took the money.

"Could you come in and get something out of the closet for me? I'm afraid I'll fall." Harry noticed that the old lady had put on her lipstick like Dorothy used to when she played dress up. It was all around her mouth instead of on it.

Mr. Kane went into the house and motioned for Harry to follow. They wiped their feet on the door-mat. It smelled funny inside, kind of like the bathroom at the state park.

Harry watched his father get a round metal cookie box down from the top of the hall closet.

"My sewing kit," said the old lady. "Blue needs a sweater for when he goes out in the cold."

Blue, a fat fluffy cat, brushed against Harry's leg. He was followed by three other cats, one skinny, one without a tail, and one that meowed continuously.

"Casper is jealous," said the old lady. "He wants a sweater, too."

Harry and his father left number twenty-two. "I do that kind of thing for some of the old folks," said Mr. Kane. "It's hard for her to get around."

Harry thought it was hard for him, too, with his cold hands and cold feet, plus scary dogs and smelly cats. It wasn't easy being a letter carrier.

Five houses later, Mr. Kane handed Harry a registered letter. "This has to be signed for," he said, ringing the doorbell.

"Who's there?" someone said.

"Mrs. Kowalski? It's the postman."

"Who's there?" someone repeated.

"It's the postman," Mr. Kane called in a louder voice. "Registered letter."

"Who's there? Who's there?" the voice continued.

"Maybe she's deaf," Harry whispered.

A man emptying garbage into the trash can by

the side of the next house called out, "There's no one home."

"Someone's answering," Mr. Kane called back.

"That's their parrot," said the man. "Noisy thing."

Mr. Kane laughed. "All in a day's work," he said to Harry.

They walked and walked. Harry thought it was worse than hiking, because at least on a hike you could eat raisins and look for bear holes and it was warm outside.

"Nobody ever offers you hot chocolate?" said Harry as they neared the end of the route.

"In the summertime, they give me lots of cold drinks," said Mr. Kane, smiling. "We're nearly done."

But they weren't. They stood on Mrs. Mandel's front porch. There was a box of groceries leaning against the door.

"I don't like it," said Mr. Kane, ringing the doorbell.

"You don't like what?" said Harry, blowing into one of his gloves.

"The groceries," said Mr. Kane, pointing to the box. "And today's newspaper. She would have taken them in."

"Maybe she's on vacation," said Harry.

"Stay here," said Mr. Kane, and he stepped off the porch and peered into one of the windows.

Harry had never seen his father run so fast. He hopped up on the porch and started jiggling the doorknob. Then he ran around the side of the house, shouting, "Harry! Follow me!"

Harry followed in time to see his father ramming his shoulder into the side door, like a fancy detective on television. The door crashed open, and his father rushed inside, through the kitchen, which felt very hot, and into the living room where a lady lay on the floor, waving her hand in the air.

"I tripped," she said weakly. "My hip."

Mr. Kane whipped a cover off the couch and draped it over the old lady. "I'm going to call nine-one-one," said Mr. Kane. "Just stay with her."

Harry sat next to the old lady on the floor. She looked very pale and had tears in her eyes. He took her hand, the way he used to take his grandma's when he visited her when she was sick.

The old lady squeezed his hand and said, "Darling," the way his grandma sometimes did. Then she jerked her head up and cried, "My oven! My pot roast!"

Harry ran into the kitchen and tugged on his father's sleeve. Mr. Kane was just giving the address into the telephone.

"She says she has a pot roast in the oven!" said Harry.

Mr. Kane reached over and switched off the oven.

"Smells ready," he said with a smile. "We'll just wait until the ambulance comes."

They went back into the living room. Mrs. Mandel waved her hand again and said, "Call my daughter." She patted the carpet, and Harry sat down next to the old lady again. She seemed to like it. She called him darling again.

Mrs. Mandel's daughter arrived a few minutes before the ambulance.

"Thank goodness you found her," she said, holding Harry's father's hand. "I called her, and when she didn't answer, I figured she was out shopping."

"My father saw her through the window," said Harry. "He broke your door."

Harry's father said he was sorry about the door, but the daughter stopped him. "My husband can fix the lock," she said, kneeling by her mother. "It's my mother that matters."

Harry heard a siren outside, and a man and a lady arrived carrying a stretcher. They carefully placed Mrs. Mandel on it and wrapped her in a special blanket.

Everyone left the house, and Mrs. Mandel's daughter turned to Mr. Kane. "Thank you again," she said. "You're a real hero. You saved my mother's life."

As she got into her car, Harry called out to her, "The pot roast is ready!"

When they got home, Harry lay down on the couch with his jacket and hat and scarf still on. His mother took off his shoes and sat next to him.

"So how did you like being a letter carrier?" she said.

Harry looked at his father. "You tell her," he said.

Mr. Kane laughed. "Today was a little unusual," he said. "We had to call the ambulance for old Mrs. Mandel. I think she broke her hip."

"Her daughter came," and Harry. "She called Daddy a hero."

"Harry was a big help," said Mr. Kane. "He stayed with Mrs. Mandel while I called nine-one-one."

"I held her hand," said Harry.

Harry's mother kissed him on the cheek. "I'm so proud of you," she said. "Do you still want to be a letter carrier when you grow up?"

Harry closed his eyes. "I don't think so," he said. "My feet still hurt."

Harry's mother patted his hand. "I'll go make dinner," she said.

"Mama?" said Harry, opening his eyes.

"What, dear?" said Mrs. Kane.

"When I grow up, I want to be a hero, just like Daddy." Harry closed his eyes again.

Mrs. Kane turned to go into the kitchen.

"Mama?" Harry called out softly.

"What, dear?" said Mrs. Kane, turning toward him.

"Pot roast," mumbled Harry. "I want pot roast for dinner." And he fell asleep.

7

Harry and the Hospital

HARRY'S MOTHER was making a cake when Grandpa called. She stopped mixing as she listened to Grandpa. Harry could tell that something was wrong, because her voice sounded funny.

"What's the matter?" said Harry, poking his head out from under his fort, which was really the kitchen table.

"Watch your head, Harry," said his mother, but she didn't tell him what was the matter.

"We'll come see her tomorrow," said Harry's mother into the receiver. "What are the hours?"

Mrs. Kane hung up the telephone, poured the batter into a cake pan, and stuck it in the oven.

"Can I lick the bowl?" said Harry.

But Harry's mother wasn't listening. Mrs. Kane had already squirted soap and run hot water into the bowl. Even Harry wouldn't lick a bowl with soap and water in it.

"You promised!" said Harry, making a face.

"I forgot," said Harry's mother, washing out the dish and putting it in the drainer.

Harry's mother must also have forgotten to put any baking powder in the cake, because it didn't rise. It was as flat as a pancake. Only Harry would eat it. Chloe and Dorothy just turned up their noses.

"Ugh," said Chloe. "Spaghetti that stuck to-gether and a cake that looks like a pancake. Can we have cookies?"

"Your mother has other things on her mind," said Mr. Kane. "Grandma is in the hospital."

"What's the matter with her?" said Harry.

"The doctor doesn't know. They're doing tests on her," said Harry's mother. "It's something to do with her heart."

"When can we visit her?" said Harry.

"Tomorrow," said Mrs. Kane. "Aunt Sara is meeting us at the hospital."

"Dorothy and I have dancing lessons tomorrow," said Chloe.

"Mrs. Peet will take you with Natasha," said Mrs. Kane. "Harry will come with us."

Harry went to his room. He was worried about Grandma. He remembered seeing a movie on television about a man in a hospital. The man had groaned a lot and had had needles stuck in his arms. He had even had something that looked like a tiny garden hose going into his nose. Harry had watched the movie until his mother came in and turned it off.

"That's not for you, Harry," she said. But Harry remembered how sad the man had looked in his

79

hospital bed. He didn't want his grandma to be sad.

Harry took out a large sheet of red construction paper. Red was Grandma's favorite color. He drew a giant circle on it, as big as his head. Then next to it, he drew an even larger circle, as big as Grandma's head. He drew two sets of eyes, and two pairs of ears, and a nose on each of the circles. Now he was ready for the most important part— the part that would make Grandma feel better in her hospital bed. Harry took out a purple crayon and drew the biggest smile that he could on the smaller circle. Then he drew an even larger smile, a gigantic smile, on the larger circle. He gave the small circle straight brown hair, like his own. Then he gave the bigger circle black curly hair, like Grandma's. He took a white crayon and stuck some bits of white hair on the black. Grandma said she was going gray, but Harry didn't think so.

Harry held up the drawing. It looked a lot like Grandma and him, but it still wasn't right. It wasn't cheerful enough, especially if Grandma had needles in her arms. Harry took some glue and squirted it all around the faces. Then he sprinkled the glue with silver and gold and purple glitter. Now the hair looked very shiny and happy, and so did the clothes. It would make Grandma smile to look at the picture.

Harry waited patiently for the picture to dry. He looked at some books. He played with his blocks. He blew on the glue, and some of the glitter flew away. At last, when he touched the sticky parts, they were dry. So he rolled up the drawing the way his teacher did in kindergarten, and he put a rubber band around it. Harry was ready to visit Grandma in the hospital. Harry was ready to make her feel better.

In the morning, Harry's mother didn't ask him what he wanted for breakfast. She just dumped some cereal into a bowl, poured some milk on it, and put it in front of him. Harry knew better than to ask her for eggs. Her face looked a little like Grumpy's, the dwarf in *Snow White and the Seven Dwarfs* who was always mad about something.

Harry ate his cereal even though his stomach felt funny. He had never visited a hospital before. It was a little like going to kindergarten for the first time, except he didn't have to stay there by himself. And he didn't have to worry about his sister Dorothy putting him in the wrong grade. His mother and father would be with him.

Except they weren't. When they got to the hospital, Aunt Sara was waiting for them inside. She was his mother's sister, and she had dark curly hair like Grandma's.

"You'll stay with Aunt Sara, Harry," said his mother. "Your father and I want to visit Grandma together."

They didn't give Harry a chance to answer. Harry watched his mother and father speak to a lady behind a big desk. The lady gave them two large pieces of cardboard. Then his parents walked past a policeman in a uniform and turned into an elevator. They were gone.

Aunt Sara said, "Come on, Harry. I'll show you around."

She took him by the hand, and they walked into a large room filled with chairs. One little boy was trying out every empty chair in the room. Harry followed him, going from chair to chair, but he made sure he held onto his rolled-up drawing that he was going to give to Grandma. Harry sat on a chair next to a lady with gray hair. She was crying into a handkerchief.

Aunt Sara came and got him. "Let's go get a snack," she said, leading him away from the old lady.

"Why is she crying?" said Harry.

"I don't know," said Aunt Sara. "Maybe a friend of hers is sick."

Harry held on tighter to his drawing. He knew how important it was to give the drawing to Grandma. He didn't want Grandpa sitting in a chair and crying.

"I have to see Grandma," said Harry.

"Children aren't allowed upstairs," said Aunt Sara. "Let's buy you a snack from one of these machines."

Harry looked at the vending machine. There

were little containers of candy bars, packages of nuts and crackers, bags of licorice, packets of cookies.

"I'll have some Reese's Pieces," said Harry. "Like Elliot in the movie *E.T.*"

Aunt Sara put the money in the slot. "B-six," she read. "Would you like to press the buttons?"

"Sure," said Harry, and before she could stop him, he pressed a P instead of a B, and then the number 6.

There was a thumping sound, and Harry reached into the machine.

"Cheese crackers?" said Harry, disappointed. He couldn't pretend he was E.T. with cheese crackers.

"You pressed the wrong letter," said Aunt Sara.

"Maybe Grandma will like them," said Harry, and he put them in his pocket.

Aunt Sara didn't say anything. She just took Harry by the hand and led him into the gift shop. "See if there's anything you'd like, Harry," she said.

While Aunt Sara looked at jewelry, Harry

looked at the toys for children. Some of them were for babies, like the rattles and bibs and stuffed animals and Raggedy Ann dolls. "I'll take this," said Harry, pointing to a robot bank.

Aunt Sara came over and looked at the price tag. "Too much money, Harry," she said. She sounded just like Harry's mother. "How about this nice pencil case?"

"Okay," said Harry. It had brightly colored dinosaurs on it, like his knapsack. He took the pencil case and put the cheese crackers inside it. They fit very nicely.

"I'm ready to see Grandma," said Harry. He still had the drawing in his hand.

Aunt Sara knelt down next to him. "I know you want to see her, Harry, but children really aren't allowed."

"Why not?" said Harry.

"Because they're too little," said Aunt Sara. "I'm sorry."

Harry thought that Aunt Sara didn't need to feel sorry. Other children might be too little, but not

Harry. Everyone said how big Harry was for his age.

"Come with me to the ladies' room," said Aunt Sara. Harry followed her into the bathroom and stood by one of the sinks. He had an idea. He would visit Grandma while Aunt Sara was going to the bathroom. By the time she combed her hair and put on her lipstick the way Harry's mother did, he would be back.

Harry left the bathroom and turned the corner. He walked past the room where the old lady was crying in her chair. He remembered watching his parents go to the elevator. He walked where they had walked, past the big desk, past the policeman in his uniform, and straight into the elevator.

Harry felt a hand on his shoulder. He heard a low voice say, "Where do you think you're going, young fellow?"

Harry looked up at the man. He wasn't smiling. "I'm going to see my Grandma Rebecca," said Harry, looking at the policeman's cap.

"Where are your parents?" said the policeman,

pressing a button. "You're not supposed to be wandering around a hospital all by yourself."

"Are you going to put me in jail?" said Harry in a small voice.

The policeman threw his hands into the air and laughed. "I don't arrest little boys visiting their grandmothers. I try to keep them safe."

They stepped out of the elevator and went over to the lady behind the big desk. "What's your grandmother's last name?" said the policeman.

Harry thought for a moment. "Rebecca," he said.

"That's her first name," said the policeman. "What's she here for?"

"She's in for some tests," said Harry.

"Tests for what?" said the policeman.

Harry knew it wasn't arithmetic or spelling. "Her heart!" said Harry. "I think it's for her heart."

The policeman said something to the lady behind the desk. Harry heard the word "heart" and then his grandma's name. The lady looked at a piece of paper and said, "The fourteenth floor."

Then the policeman took off his jacket and hung it behind the lady's chair. He wiped his forehead with a large handkerchief and took Harry's hand. Harry felt very safe with his small hand in the policeman's big one.

Harry looked up at the policeman. "My daddy is as tall as you are," he said.

"Is he, now?" said the policeman, leading Harry into the elevator. "Let's go find your grandmother."

Harry watched the policeman press the number fourteen button. He had big muscles that rippled when he moved his arm.

Harry tugged on the policeman's hand. "My daddy is as tall as you are," he said. "But I think you have bigger muscles. Maybe policemen need bigger muscles than letter carriers."

The policeman laughed very loudly. "I'm not a policeman. I'm a security guard," he said. "This is our floor. Let's go find your parents."

It didn't take long to find Grandma's room. They walked straight to the noisiest room on the floor. Harry heard his mother say, "Thank goodness, it's Harry." Aunt Sara looked as if she was going to faint.

"Where on earth did you go, Harry?" said his mother. "Aunt Sara said one minute you were in the bathroom, and the next you were gone. We were so frightened!"

"I had to give something to Grandma," said Harry. "I'm sorry I scared you."

The security guard spoke up. "He said he was looking for his grandmother. I told him he couldn't go running around a hospital alone."

"And here I am," said a small voice from the other side of the room.

Harry ran over to the bed. It was just his grandma with no needles and no tubes, only a little plastic bracelet around her wrist. Grandpa was holding her hand.

"I needed to see you, Grandma," said Harry. He took the rubber band off the drawing and unrolled it. Some flakes of glitter scattered onto Grandma's bed, but Grandma didn't seem to mind.

Harry held up the drawing. "It's you and me," he said.

Grandma smiled. Maybe it wasn't as big a smile as the one in the picture, but her eyes crinkled in the corners the way they always did.

"I feel better already," Grandma announced, holding out her arms.

"I thought you would," said Harry, hugging Grandma.

"Let's go down now," said Harry's mother.

"Good-bye, Grandma," said Harry. "I'll see you when you get home."

"Good-bye, Harry," said Grandma. "Thank you for the beautiful picture. I'll hang it on the wall."

"Grandma?" said Harry.

"Yes, darling?" said Grandma.

"Can you save me the plastic bracelet?"

"Of course," said Grandma, smiling her crinkly smile.

Then Harry took his mother's hand, and they walked over to the elevator. Harry's mother let him press the button.

8

Harry Grows Up

I<small>T WAS</small> H<small>ARRY</small>'<small>S</small> first springtime in his new neighborhood. Springtime meant a lot to Harry. He could play outdoors, in the front yard or backyard of his new house, with his new friend Benjamin. Sometimes, if it was warm enough outside, he could take off his jacket. He could even look for crocuses with his sisters, Chloe and Dorothy. Whoever found the first flower poking out of the ground won.

Springtime also meant it was Harry's mother's birthday. On Saturday, Harry's father was giving her a pizza party. Some of the neighbors were invited, and Harry's grandma and grandpa, and Aunt Sara, too.

Harry and Chloe and Dorothy were sitting outside on the front steps.

"We'll make her a beautiful card," said Chloe.

"With glitter," said Dorothy.

"Again?" said Harry. "We do that every time. This year I want to buy her a present."

"With what?" said Chloe. "We don't have any money."

"We'll make some," said Harry. "We'll have a grown-up store outside."

"But what will we sell?" said Dorothy. She picked up a rock next to the step she was sitting on.

"I'll think of something," said Harry. Harry was only in kindergarten, but he had a good imagination.

The screen door opened. "Do you want anything to eat?" said Harry's mother. Harry could smell her before he could see her. She had on his favorite perfume.

"Tea Rose," said Harry.

"To eat?" said his mother, laughing.

"Of course not," said Harry. "You're wearing Tea Rose, and we'll have some Goldfish to eat."

"Coming up," said his mother, shutting the screen door behind her.

"I've got it!" said Harry, jumping up off the porch so quickly that Dorothy almost dropped the rock she was holding on her toe.

"What?" said Chloe.

"Perfume!" said Harry. "We'll make the most beautiful perfume in the world, and everybody will buy it."

"I don't know, Harry," said Chloe. She had the same look on her face that she had when Harry tried to make her taste Rocky Road ice cream. Doubtful.

"It will be easy!" said Harry, but he shushed everybody because he could smell his mother at the door again.

"Goldfish," said Mrs. Kane. "And juice boxes." She put the boxes on the porch.

"Do you have any tiny bottles we could use?" said Harry, munching on a handful of Goldfish.

"For what?" said Mrs. Kane.

"It's a secret," said Chloe. "We promise we won't make a mess."

"I'll go see," she said, heading back inside.

"I have another idea!" said Dorothy, jumping up from the porch so quickly that Harry spilled some of his Goldfish.

"What?" said Harry, eating the spilled Goldfish because the porch looked very clean.

"Rocks!" said Dorothy, holding up her rock.

"Rocks in the head," said Chloe, twirling a finger at her forehead.

"Painted rocks to sell!" said Dorothy excitedly. "For paperweights."

"And bookends!" said Harry.

Dorothy and Chloe went to the backyard looking for rocks. Dorothy made Chloe pick them up, because sometimes bugs crawled out from under them. They collected six rocks from the back of the garden and went inside to wash them off.

Meanwhile, Harry collected bottles. His mother gave him a set of old perfume containers and a few miniature jam jars. Harry emptied out a bottle of screws from his tool box that was really a baby food jar, and that made seven perfume bottles in all.

While Chloe and Dorothy painted rocks in Chloe's bedroom, Harry shut himself in the bathroom with his bottles. He took the basin that his mother used to wash out her panty hose, and poured in two capfuls of his favorite shampoo. It was herbal and smelled like Christmas trees. Then he squirted some dishwashing liquid into the basin, the stuff his mother used for hand washing. The commercial said it smelled like sunlight.

"Sunlight is nice," said Harry, squirting a little more.

Harry reached for a can of cleanser from behind the toilet. He always liked the smell of it when his father washed pots with it.

"Just a sprinkle," said Harry, dusting the basin with it. Then he added a capful of lemon disinfectant. His mother always said she liked the smell.

Harry opened the door a crack. He stuck his head out, looking for his mother, but he could hear her singing downstairs.

He ran into his mother's room and pulled a stool over to his mother's dresser.

"I'll just borrow a little," said Harry, taking his mother's bottle of Tea Rose. He put two drops of Tea Rose into the basin and returned it to his mother's dresser.

Harry sniffed at the basin. The smell wasn't quite right yet. Harry thought for a moment. Then he had his best idea yet. If he put some of his father's aftershave cologne in the perfume, men could wear it, too!

Harry sprinkled two drops of Brut into the basin, a drop of Stetson, and some water.

"Cowboys are nice," said Harry, and he took the end of his toothbrush and stirred with it as if he was making a cake.

There was a knock on the door. "Are you done?" whispered Chloe. Harry let his sisters in because he knew they could pour better.

"Smells good!" said Dorothy, sniffing at the basin. Chloe dipped the bottles into the liquid until they were full. She screwed the tops on. Then she tried to rinse out the basin. The more water she added, the more bubbles appeared.

"I hope this perfume doesn't bubble up on the skin," said Chloe, a worried look on her face.

"I hope it doesn't rain," said Dorothy as she watched Chloe wash away the last of the bubbles.

"It won't," said Harry, tapping a finger to his mouth. He was busy thinking up a name for his perfume and aftershave cologne.

"Smells good!" shouted Harry.

"That's what *I* said," said Dorothy.

Harry instructed Chloe to write out a sign:

HARRY KANE'S SMELLS-GOOD PERFUME
OR AFTERSHAVE COLOGNE

Chloe added the word *unisex,* because she was in the third grade and remembered that her mother went to a unisex hairdresser that cut men's and women's hair.

The next day after school, Chloe dragged an old table from the garage to the grass by the sidewalk.

It worked out perfectly, because Aunt Sara was watching them while Mrs. Kane got her hair done, and Aunt Sara promised to keep the store a secret.

Aunt Sara read the sign:

HARRY KANE'S UNISEX SMELLS-GOOD PERFUME
OR AFTERSHAVE COLOGNE

Underneath, it, in smaller letters, Chloe had printed, PAINTED ROCKS FOR SALE.

"Boy!" said Aunt Sara. "You've been busy! How much is everything?"

Harry looked at Chloe. Chloe shrugged her shoulders. "Pay as you wish," said Chloe in a grown-up voice. "The proceeds go to our mother's birthday present."

"In that case," said Aunt Sara, "I'll take a perfume for me, and an aftershave for Uncle Peter, and a rock for my desk." She handed Harry a five-dollar bill. "Is this enough?" she said.

"Wow!" said Harry, handing the bill to Chloe. "We're rich!"

Chloe was more businesslike. She took the rock

and wrapped it in newspaper, and she put the perfume bottles in a plastic bag.

"Be sure to wear our perfume to Mom's party," said Chloe.

"Of course," said Aunt Sara, and she took her packages and went inside.

Their neighbor Mrs. Peet drove up in her car and walked over to the store.

"Just what I need!" said Mrs. Peet, selecting the baby jar of perfume because Chloe had drawn pretty flowers on the label.

She gave Chloe a dollar. "Is this enough?"

"That's great," said Chloe. "Remember to wear your perfume to the party."

"I will," said Mrs. Peet. "I'll put some on Natasha, too."

Grandpa pulled into the driveway and honked his horn. "What's up?" he said, unrolling his window.

"Would you like to buy some perfume for Mom's birthday party present?" said Harry, running over to the window.

"It's unisex!" called Chloe. "You can wear it, too!"

Grandpa bought one for himself and one for Grandma, too, and he promised to wear it to the party.

It was getting dark outside. Harry and Dorothy dragged the table back into the garage while Chloe counted the money.

"Ten dollars!" said Chloe excitedly. They went inside to tell Aunt Sara.

"Would you like me to pick up a nice tape for your mother?" said Aunt Sara. "She likes classical jazz."

"That would be great," said Chloe, and she handed Aunt Sara the money.

"And some wrapping paper," said Harry.

"And a card," said Dorothy.

Aunt Sara looked at the ten dollars. "Why don't you make your mother a card? She'd like that. And I'll make sure the present is wrapped."

That night, Harry cut a heart out of pink construction paper. He wrote *Harry* in very large letters across the front of it. Then, taking out an old Valentine card, he copied the word *Love* underneath his name. He took out the prettiest bottle of Harry Kane's Unisex Smells-Good Perfume that he had left, and he wrapped it in a piece of the comics from the Sunday newspaper. Harry looked at the present. It was a little messy but very colorful. He looked at the card. His heart was crooked and looked more like a squashed triangle. But he had made the card, all by himself, and he had wrapped the present, all by himself, and he had mixed the perfume, all by himself. Harry looked in the mirror above his dresser. He thought his face looked a little older and his eyes looked a little smarter. Harry was getting bigger. Harry was growing up.

On the morning of the birthday party, Harry's mother wasn't allowed to do a thing. At first, she sat and read the newspaper. But Mr. Kane found her biting her nails and sent her outside for a walk.

Chloe vacuumed the living room while Dorothy and Harry sprayed and dusted. Then they set the table with pretty paper plates, and everybody helped Mr. Kane make a huge salad. Harry was very good at ripping lettuce because he used to do it for Personality. Finally, Mr. Kane ordered the pizza, one plain, one with mushrooms, and one with anchovies for the grown-ups, which Harry wouldn't try because it smelled too fishy.

The doorbell rang, and Aunt Sara and Uncle Peter walked in the door. Harry ran over to his aunt and hugged her, sniffing at her neck as she bent down.

"I forgot," his aunt whispered, her face turning a little red. "I forgot to wear your wonderful perfume."

"It's okay," said Harry in a grown-up voice.

Harry turned to Uncle Peter.

"I forgot, too," said Uncle Peter hastily.

"It's okay," Harry repeated. He thought Uncle Peter's face looked a little red, too.

The doorbell rang again, and Mrs. Peet arrived with Natasha. Harry took their coats, draping them over his arm the way he had watched his father do.

"Did you remember to wear the perfume?" he asked them.

Mrs. Peet clapped a hand to her mouth. "I completely forgot," she said.

"You were holding it in your hand," said Natasha. "You picked your other one." Mrs. Peet gave her a funny look, and Natasha didn't say any more.

Harry carried the coats upstairs and put them across his parents' bed. He heard the doorbell ring and ran downstairs to greet Grandma and Grandpa. Grandma would remember to wear the perfume, and so would Grandpa.

Harry hugged his grandmother. She smelled very sweet, but she smelled like baby powder. She didn't smell like Harry Kane's Unisex Smells-Good Perfume. He hugged his grandfather. Grandpa smelled fresh, as if he had just shaved. But he didn't smell like Harry Kane's Unisex Smells-Good Aftershave.

"You didn't wear it?" said Harry sadly.

"I'm saving it," said Grandma. "For Aunt Cora's wedding."

"Me, too," muttered Grandpa.

Harry ran upstairs. He threw himself on top of his bed and buried his head in his brontosaurus pillow. He lay there for a few minutes. How could Aunt Sara and Uncle Peter and Mrs. Peet and Natasha and Grandma and Grandpa all forget to wear his wonderful perfume? He sat up. Unless they weren't telling the truth. Harry pictured all of them with very, very, very long noses, like Pinocchio's.

Harry reached for the comic-strip-wrapped present sitting on his desk. He ripped off the paper. He unscrewed the cap and pressed his finger against the opening. When his finger was wet with perfume, he wiped it on his cheeks, the way he watched his father do after a shave.

It felt . . . slimy. Like squishy soap at the bottom of a soap dish.

Harry sniffed. He held his finger to his nose and sniffed again. It smelled funny. Not half as good as Grandma's baby powder or Grandpa's aftershave or his mother's Tea Rose. He held the bottle to his nose. It smelled disgustingly, sickeningly awful, almost like the cottage cheese when it was in his mother's refrigerator too long.

Harry went into the bathroom and closed the door. He poured the perfume down the sink and ran the hot water until all the bubbles had disappeared.

When Harry opened the bathroom door, he could hear his mother's voice calling out, "Is it safe to come in now?" He heard everyone laughing and cheering. His mother sounded happy. She wouldn't like it if Harry was sad.

Harry picked up his heart-shaped card and walked downstairs. His father was paying the pizza man in the hallway.

"Harry!" said his mother, holding out her arms. "Aunt Sara tells me you and Chloe and Dorothy bought me a present, all by yourselves."

"And I made you this," said Harry, handing her the card and snuggling into his mother's arms.

"How beautiful!" said Mrs. Kane, kissing him on the cheek. "Daddy says you were a big help with the party. And Chloe says it was your idea to have a store and earn some money."

"I'm growing up," said Harry proudly.

"You certainly are," said his mother, kissing him

once more on the cheek. "Now go and wash up, sweetheart, so you can eat your pizza. Your face smells a little funny."

Harry went into the bathroom one more time. He looked into the mirror. He was still Hurricane Harry, but he was definitely taller, maybe a whole inch. His eyes looked very, very smart. After all, this year Harry had moved to a new house. He had survived being put in the wrong grade by his sister Dorothy. He had made new friends in kindergarten. He had buried Personality. He had cheered up Grandma in the hospital.

Harry picked up a washcloth and ran it under the water. Then he rubbed it with soap. He scrubbed his cheeks hard until they were wet and shiny, and he wiped his face with a towel.

Harry took one last look in the mirror. He was taller, and he was smarter. He was so grown-up that he might, he just might, try a piece of pizza with an anchovy on it. Even if it smelled fishy.